THE SECRET ROOM

MOHD SAIF

ISBN 979-888569243-4

Contents

About The Author   v

About The Book   vii

1. Chapter 1   1

About The Author

Mohd Saif

Mohammed Saifuddin, better known by his pen name Sεif is an author of fictional, non fictional stories and screenwriter.

About The Book

The secret room is a mystery fictional novel which talks about a secret service which was planned by a father and fulfilled by his son

ONE

Long ago ....

There was a city named Hanoi in Vietnam. Where a man named Lee Paulin used to live with his family. His wife named Hang moon. The son named as Jade Paulin. Lee Paulin was one of the top sci-fi. His house consists of a secret security alert which was designed by himself.

From childhood Paulin had patriotism towards his nation. and his dream was to join the army and protect the nation. But due to his weakness in his legs a disease named myasthenia gravis. He could not follow his dream also he was good in studies. In the end he chose the path of science and became a research fellow of the secret service. by which we can help the people but don't show the identity so he made everything that a beginner needs to be a perfect secret agent and thought to fulfil his dream with the help of his son Jade Paulin.

As The days passed "the secret room" was ready but the details map, formula and guide of how it work s was not ready and jade Paulin son of lee Paulin was also in science and he was the topper of the school at end of the 10th standard so, one day jade Paulin father lee Pauling said to his son that "I will give you a gift on your upcoming birthday which you will remember in your whole life, but before that you have to prepare yourself as a patriot then his son agree and start to be patriot. Then his father completes the research and succeeded to invent the secret room with all maps, layouts information and he prepared all maps layouts how it is works as a guide and plan to give to his son on his birthday and he keep that guide in his locker with a four number pin.

It was the day of his son and everything is ready for his birthday present and mean while he was climbing the stairs suddenly his leg slips and he roll down from the stairs of second floor to ground floor with a severe injury on his head and he was admitted to the hospital. when his mother and son asked the doctor.

And the doctor said "due to severe injury on the head he lost his memory, in other words it is called traumatic amnesia. Due to the fact that he has forgotten all things, there is a chance of getting back all memories or not we can't say. Mother heard all the things and she was shocked then she fell unconscious. Then doctor said if any movement we will inform you. After some days his father discharged from the hospital and back to home. Then his son asked dad what was the present you planned for me. Then his father replied to her son in a tentative way "what present i didn't recognize any thing And for whose birthday was the present for ? I don't remember. Jade Paulin was a little bit dejected and astonished. Then he asked his mother about that. Then his mother replied "your dad never shared any kind of information related to his research and works.
Jade was confused about what to do......

Then his son starts thinking and searching the present planned by his father

He searches every single corner of his father's room. Then he finds a locker which contains a four-digit pin which was locked by his father. Then he tries the vehicle number but he couldn't. At the end of two attempts, he will be unsuccessful to enter the correct pin. And a last chance will be remaining. If he doesn't enter the correct pin this time everything will be burnt inside the locker.

Then he starts asking his mother about his dad's nature and hobbies and everything. After listening to his father's life stories and hobbies and the nature of his father, he concludes a common thing that here father is a patriot.

Then he starts searching of the nation codes, pins, and every four-digit pin code related to Vietnam. After searching whole night next day on the next day, he found the four-digit code which is country code by which Vietnam is represents in the (ISO) international organization for standardization

Then he went to that safe he was full of terror. He enters the code (3166-2) then he hears a sound in the safe. His heart beat was gradually increasing suddenly the door of the safe opened. His face was full of surprise and happiness and his joy was inexpressible. Then he checked out the locker and found a letter with a book.

Jade's mind was full of questions but there was the only man to clarify his doubt and he was not in condition to clarify. So, he took the letter and book to his room. Then the next morning he took that letter and started reading the things which were written in the letter.

The letter....

Dear son,

First of all, many more happy returns of the day. the present i am going to give you is better than a BMW or Audi and it is everlasting and the present is in that book. Wait first to read these instructions properly then open it.
*From now on you are going to protect our nation in a disguise which is unknown means you're going to be the secret agent and head of the secret room.
*And you will find the directions and key of the secret room in the book.
*The secret room is between you and me, if you say this to anyone it will no longer be a secret room.
*And when you enter the secret room. There is an instructor which is totally designed by me, it will help you to become a perfect secret agent
"Now you can open the book"
"the secret room is all yours my boy"

I hope you will full fill my dream by protecting our nation (Mr Jade Paulin the secret agent)
Hope you like my present 'all the best for your upcoming era and I hope you make me proud!'
Then he takes that book and opens it then it is written in that. Welcome to the secret service
And the secret room is built in my room and when you enter my room you will find a library where there is a book. named "mystery within"

When you take that book you will find a button. When you press that button, you will find a door and it has a specially designed key that is at the centre of the book. When you enter inside it will close automatically and the instructor will tell you everything from there.
"All the best for your future my boy"

Then he runs back to his mom with the key and tells the whole story to her and at the end he tells her to keep it a secret and she has to live without him for some days or months and comes back with a book to his dad's room.
Then for the first time he enters the secret room. suddenly when he enters inside a huge cage fall on him and capture him and after sometime a robot designed by his father comes near to the cage and asks him what is the code Then Jade thinks for a while and replies 3166 then he removes him and ask him to forgive. After a while. the robot asks the Jade that are you ready for your training then jade replies "yes always"

Then your training starts from today. Then a door opens. Jade was full of excitement and a little confused that the robot would be going in.
And in the six months training he will be taught how to use guns, missiles, snipers, cars, truck, every vehicle even a helicopter. And he will be also taught about hacking, digital techniques, how to defend himself by enemies and every professional thing that a secret agent should have and Main thing taught in training is how to hide their identity. And how to prepare for a mission.

After six months of hard work and training he will buy him back to the secret room and then shown the most interesting part of the secret room the instructor robot gives him a letter and a key and ask him to read when you go out of this secret room and first to open the secret agents room. Then he opens the room with the help of that key

When he enters to agents' room, he will think that is it real then robot says "sir the equipment that you need, you can take when you want" The room was full of guns, missiles, grenades, smokes, and sophisticated tools which are hard to identify by the people And they were made as no machine can track them and specialised sceptring's shoes, bullet proof jackets, which look like a normal one.

After looking at all of these he comes out from the secret room. And opens the letter given by his instructor. The letter as follows.

Dear son (Jade Paulin)

I hope you learned and enjoyed the training .And I am writing this to give you. your first secret mission and this mission is only to save and protect our nation that the main person of the higher law of nation is planning of supply drugs, nuclear bomb testing and trying to take 90 percent of the money which is only for the welfare of the nation so you to kill him. And there is huge party on the 1st of upcoming month. so, I have already booked a pass you will find that pass in the book "mystery within" be prepared for the mission i had made you a secret agent. And i have arranged you the thing up to the party from there you are going to do by yourself

What you learned in your training and come back with

success without showing your identity and don't worry about money. When you return back to the secret room there are lots of money by which you can enjoy your whole life.

I know after reading this your mind is full of doubts & questions leave them let's clarify them after mission there is pass and photo in the cover get ready my boy makes our nation proud without identity
" all the best my boy"

After a short time of waiting the day has come and the jade was full of focus and excitement in his eyes and ready with every equipment used for the mission and the design was specially design by his father which was normal to see but modified from in., he was ready to go and in time less than 15-20 minutes he reached there. He was ready to enter. The person who was supposed to kill arrived there and whispered with his guards in the car that he will be in the room for some time because he is feeling tired. but Jade listens it with help of specially designed Bluetooth which can hear sound up to 2kms

After whispering in his ears, he enters with 10 guards inside the hall to his restroom which was made with concrete and after he enters it automatically locks and have 4-digit pin. The person was on his way to the room. Then suddenly Jade calls sir please wait then he takes the powder which can only see through his specialized specs and shakes his hand with that person and says "sir myself jade Paulin can i have photo with you. He replies yeah! Sure, then he will go back and the person of high law enters pin with those hands

Then he enters in and the door locks automatically then Jade goes near to the door then he picks up mutant and pistols from his shirt kill them within 10 minutes without sound then he sees the keyboard of the safe with the spects and open and enters in and the person in will be in bathtub and when he see him he press the emergency button and smile by saying whole army of this area will be her in 10 min .Then he shoots him and kill him and fill the whole room with grenades and connect it with the door so when they open the doors boom!

Then he sends all the innocent people out by exit within 10 minutes then the army arrives there opens that door and boom! And these grenades were only for made for that specific area destruction and mission was successful without loss of a single life
And his father gets back his memory due to continuous medications
Then his son takes his father to his room and says all the things he learned and did in the mission and his father felt proud and started crying then calmed him down. After that he started asking all the questions which were in his mind.
Jade's dad replied "When you think you will find those answer and Everything is connected my boy"